DATE			

A Son of War

'Can you do this?'

Mary turned to the house, took a step or so back, a skip forward, dipped onto her hands and swung her legs up against the wall, swung them it seemed to the mesmerised Joe through the most perfect arc, the legs lazily tracking each other into the air, and with a grace that winded him. He stared at the two small shiny red clogs neatly nailed on the grimy brick and saw the bare legs with the skirt now dangling towards the ground.

A year or so before, before the move to Water Street, when he had been a full member of the Market Hill gang, the rather older Harrison girls, twins, who led it, had sometimes teased the boys by being bad. Joe had been left frustrated and pining for days after these rare encounters with the incomprehensible. Now he had the same hot feeling of wanting to do something urgently but what it was he did not know.

The Harrison girls had also done handstands against a wall. But they had tucked their skirts into their knickers.

That brief snap of memory was frazzled by this posed, erect figure, polished red clogs gleaming side by side, bare legs, green knickers, the skirt all but covering her upside-down face. And she stayed like that. For more than a second or two. Joe was helpless, dizzy with awe. It was beyond him yet it possessed him.

He could hold it no longer. Unmistakable. The hot clart of it on his cold thigh. Yet still he stood there. Then she reversed the action and the feet nudged lightly against the wall, the legs swung down, just as gracefully, and she stood and turned and smiled at him and saw her applause in his face.

He nodded and swallowed the saliva that had gathered in the well of his mouth. He had to take on trust that she would not vanish from the earth as he hobbled as fast as he could to the messy stinkhole just vacated by boozy Kettler to try to sort out his own mess.

How could he get her to do that handstand against the wall again?

—〜—

Speed was a hero and sometimes a friend. His advantage in age was almost three full years. One of Joe's multitude of ambitions was to be as old as Speed, to be ten, to be as brave as Speed, to be as bad and as dangerous as Speed. To have Speed in him. He envied his slight squint and tried to copy it.

Speed ate scrunts. He even ate the stalks. He chewed candlewax for gum. Speed drove cattle down Water Street and New Street to the pens at the station. Speed smoked dog ends when he found them in his scourings of the gutter. Most grown-ups shouted at him and Speed shouted back and then ran. Speed led the Water Street younger gang in stone fights and raids on other streets. He would go to the tip and always come back with something good that just needed holding under the tap. Speed swore and then crossed himself. Nobody, said Speed, was better than the Pope. Speed's daddy was in hospital because of the war but if anybody referred to it Speed hit them. Some days, market days, he just did not go to school. Speed boasted that his big brother Alistair would be lucky not to go to Borstal before he got called up. Joe's daddy called Speed 'a little warrior' and always seemed to be smiling at him. Speed said things to Sam that Joe would never dare.

'Put them on.'

Speed was reluctant. The gloves looked too expensive. But Mr Richardson was an idol outpointed only by his brother Alistair. He pulled on the glossy gloves and felt his fist disappear as Sam tugged the laces tight across his thin wrist.

'Now remember you're bigger, and remember you're older.'

Speed nodded. The gloves were unwieldy and unnecessary. His fist felt imprisoned.

'Just some gentle sparring,' said Sam. 'OK?' He looked over to Joe who was experiencing an unexpected sense of calm. Perhaps because Sam had just sprung this on them and he had had no time to work up a funk. And he could see that Speed was uncomfortable in the gloves. And Sam was there.

'Seconds out. Ding!'

The boys came towards each other cautiously, Joe adopting some semblance of the classic English stance – left foot forward, head tucked behind his right glove, left glove feinting for an opening. Speed was hopeless. In a fight he just flailed away until it was over. He could not play at it.

Joe saw that Mary had come out into the yard. She leaned against the window-ledge as she had the other day. Joe danced, just a touch, on the balls of his feet and waved his left glove more emphatically. He tried a punch. Speed let it land on his shoulder. Joe glanced at Mary and shot out a straight left.

'Good lad!'

Joe burrowed his head further into the protecting right glove and found that he was advancing. Speed was waving his arms, almost as if he were trying to shake off the bulbous impediments. Joe jabbed out the left once or twice, did not connect, looked good. Mary had not moved.

Speed swung his left hand in a looping swipe that landed on Joe's glove and rocked him. But instead of alarm, he felt fired up. He could tell that Speed was not going to hurt him. He had seen it in the pleading look his hero had cast to Sam.

Joe skipped a little more then flung his right hand forward. Speed caught it between his two gloves, as if it were a ball, and when Joe tried to free it, his hand slipped out and Speed stood there holding the empty glove like a trophy.

'First time I've seen that!' Sam laughed and Joe hoped it was not he who was being laughed at.

'Can I stop now, Mr Richardson?' said Speed.

'You're hardly warmed up.'

'But I don't want to fight him, Mr Richardson.'

Joe was much relieved. The stoppage had jolted him into the realisation that he was pushing his luck. But, for Mary's sake, he tried to look keen.

'This is boxing,' said Sam.

Speed shook his head. You had a fight because you meant it. You could mean it so badly that you thought you wanted to murder somebody. Sometimes it was hard to stop when it was over. This with the gloves was just no good.

'He can hit me and I won't hit back.'

Joe gave a little jig to show willing.

Sam ruffled Speed's cropped hair. 'You're a real 'un,' he said, and unlaced the boy's gloves. Joe looked on carefully. He remembered Speed saying, 'I wish thy father was my father,' and it had made him proud.

Liberated, Speed muttered a lie of excuse and fled.

'You'll have to make do with me again,' said Sam, and he coaxed and coached Joe for a respectable ten minutes before taking the gloves into the house.

At last Joe could go across to Mary. He had a light sweat, a sheen against the cold, and it gave him a swagger.

'Bella wants to see Blackie,' said Mary.

Bella had not been seen since before Christmas, much to Joe's relief. The big over-clumsy girl whom Kettler scorned as 'backward' and 'mental' had ceased to worry him after he had come into possession of the kitten Blackie. Bella was besotted by Blackie and a promise that she could hold her never failed to check the mauling play with which she had unsettled the much smaller Joe. He was still nervous of her.

'Mammy says she's very badly.' Joe lowered his voice, as his mother did when she spoke of illness. She had referred to it in oblique and embarrassed snatches so that Joe came to the conclusion that Bella was a leper – he had heard a forceful sermon on lepers – and if he so much as touched her or let her breathe at him he would be covered in boils and sores and die.

Part of Ellen's reluctance to tell the boy the truth – aside from her ineradicable conviction that a host of adult truths, especially on personal matters, were not to be shared with or imposed on children – was that she feared she would reveal her anger.

It was criminal, Ellen thought, and said as much to Sam, that Bella's mother Madge should insist that she house and nurse her sister riddled with TB when everyone with any sense knew that the disease fed on such intense crowding in a small damp space. She had read the doctor in the *Cumberland News* who was agitated that so many people turned their back on the obvious ways of alleviating the current Wigton rampage of tuberculosis. But Madge did not take the *Cumberland News* and Ellen could not engineer a discussion without giving offence.

Influenced by the social rigidities of a childhood with an aspiring aunt, Ellen had no truck with unannounced neighbourliness. You were friendly but not familiar, not dropping in without knocking, not sticking your nose into private business, not giving advice unasked for. But it said clearly in the paper that the sanatorium only ten miles away

Joe glanced up, alert. Looked from one to the other. Saw them looking steadily at each other. But they were not angry. He always knew when they were angry. So. It was all right.

'He starts on Tuesday,' said Ellen.

CHAPTER SIX

Sam all but marched Joe down the street. Partly to beat the weather. Partly, though, because he liked to push the boy now and then and enjoyed the child's determination to meet the challenge. After trying to match the length of his father's step, Joe had fallen into unsatisfactory syncopation. But he squared his shoulders and mimicked his father's bearing. One or two people noticed and remarked, 'Like his dad, now,' and Joe felt proud. Already around the town he was called 'Sam's lad' by the older men, although grown-up women still called him 'Ellen's boy'.

Sam's copper hair was still army short with a touch of Brylcreem to keep every follicle in formation. Joe's copper was beginning to lose the deep hue and was becoming merely ginger, even rather brown in places. But the blue eyes were father and son.

'Fine lad,' said Henry Allen, the bookmaker, who came across the street to walk with them. Sam took the compliment. Joe pretended to ignore it but felt a tickle of pleasure shimmer through him.

'What brings you out?'

'Good business practice, Sam. Something that has to be learned.'

Henry's sallow face was blank white with cold save for the redness of his nose. He was wrapped up for a Russian winter.

'These landlords, you see, Sam, they do me a favour when racing's on. Collect the bets. Or let Tommy' – his runner – 'come in and collect them. All definitely illegal, Sam. Outside the law and an offence. You can come to the bookmaker's office but the bookmaker's office can't come to you. Sorry business, Sam. Law made to be broken. So when the racing's off, I make a point of going into the pub, buying a round or two. Good business practice.'

He coughed, a dry scratchy cough that felt sore just to listen to it.

'Stomach bad enough. Ulcers forewarned. Chest joining in,' he said, and they had to stop while he coughed it out.

They were near Market Hill, early Saturday afternoon, enough people for it to be embarrassing. Henry walked to the front of the big house owned by the manager of the Lion and Lamb and coughed into the wall. Sam and Joe waited.

He came back, watery-eyed. 'Terrible thing,' he said, 'bad health.' He diverted matters to Joe. 'You look after your health. What's he going to be, Sam?'

'Tell him.'

'World champion,' said Joe, 'or,' and this came, new, from nowhere, 'have a band.'

Both men laughed at the innocent unreality of it and Joe knew he had pleased his father. He had to. And in that moment he believed what he said.

'What they come out with,' said Harry. He excavated the layers of his clothing, finally found his money pocket and fingered through the change until he found a sixpence. 'Don't spend it all at once.'

'Thank you, Mr Allen.'

'See you, Sam. Frost's got all the courses now. Not a horse moving in all the land.'

The bookmaker peeled off to continue his good business practice in the Blackamoor Inn. Sam and Joe swung on to the crest of Market Hill and made for the house in which Ellen and Joe had taken refuge during his war years. Joe still treated it as a home. Sam rarely came to it without remembering the man who was himself, who, less than a year ago, after the eternity of the slow return from Burma, had bounded up the steps on a mild morning to reclaim his wife and child and past.

This time he went in by the back door. Joe had already darted ahead and the door was ajar. Just as Leonard and Grace had been as parents to Ellen, so they had been as grandparents to Joe and he took all the leeway they gave him.

Sam had picked the time carefully so that he could have a quiet talk with Leonard, who was as near as he got to a confidant in Wigton.

Grace had made them a pot of tea. She had softened towards Sam since his second return but Sam knew that it was because she thought he was weak for not going to Australia. She had been looking forward to having Ellen back in her house, skivvying (as Sam had cruelly put it to Ellen's distress), and Joe as the plaything. But the piano had brought Joe back and Ellen was grateful once again to the magnificently coiffed, deep-bosomed Grace, lady of this castle of a house on the hill. Now, superior in resolution to a man she had always rather feared, Grace felt well compensated. Sam tried to block it out. Of those few who had joshed him about that damned turning back at Carlisle station, only Grace had got under his skin. He was extra polite to her. She spotted that, and she enjoyed that, too.

Leonard opened with the offer of a cigarette. Both of them were on Capstan Full Strength. The semi-basement kitchen was an uncomfortable place for confidences but it was the best that could be found outside the luck of an empty snug in one of the pubs. And you could not always afford to drink. Grace was upstairs planted in her hauled him to within inches so that their faces almost touched. 'Always respect your mammy and daddy now. Won't you? I want you to promise.'

Joe attempted to look for support but Colin had him in a grip. 'Promise,' he said.

'Good lad.' Colin let him go. Joe smiled at his mother as if he had given her a present with the promise and she looked so happy he knew that he had.

'We'd better be off,' said Sam.

'Joe hasn't done his practice,' said Grace, swiftly.

'He plays the piano,' Ellen explained to Colin, trying to neutralise her tone. 'Well, he's starting to.'

'A musician in the family!' Colin looked amazed.

'I can play three scales and two tunes,' said Joe, flustered with the excitement of it all. The moment the boast left his lips he was aware of the ice blast from Ellen.

'Give us a listen then.'

With a glance of what he hoped was sufficient apology to his mother – but she would not satisfy him with a forgiving look – he went to the piano and performed the scale of C major with both hands.

'That's terrific!' said Colin. 'No flannel. Can you do another?'

Sam went out. They would think he had gone to the lavatory. They could think what they wanted. Two more minutes of Colin and he would have hit the ceiling.

In the cobbled yard he leaned against a wall opposite the row of run-down cottages from each of which came a glow of gas-light intimating a luxuriance of cosiness. He took his time over a cigarette and damped down that sudden flare of intense dislike. The man would go soon enough, he reassured himself. A visit was a visit. He would just have to shut his eyes and his ears and block out the effect the man had on Ellen and Joe. Sam shook his head to rid himself of the images of his wife and son, the one clinging admiringly to this worthless man, the other straining himself to please.

He ground the butt into the cobbles with an over-emphatic twist of his heel. He could drag it out no longer.

Only Grace was in the room, in the same seat, forlorn, her subjects all deserted her.

'Colin wanted a walk up the street,' she explained.

Sam felt a rare sympathy for her.

'So what did you make of him, Grace?' The boldness of tone and question caused no offence. She was deep in the well of her past.

'He is my nephew,' she said, separating one word from the other with a pronounced gap that made them sound like a forced confession. 'He is my only brother's son. Whatever I make of him.'

'What did you think of his father?' It was a question that Sam had wanted to ask in his first weeks with Ellen. Not then. Not since. But now.

'I thought the world of him.'

Her voice was low and it vibrated with sorrow. Her head was bent and she seemed to be talking more to herself than to Sam. And that proud imperial figure lowered her head.

'I always understood,' said Sam, after a pause that indicated she would say no more unprompted, 'that he was a bit of a black sheep, Grace. Word was you were glad to get rid of him.'

'He was a black sheep.' She nodded grim assent. 'But I would have done anything to stop him running away.'

'Why did he?'

'Because he was weak!' She was abrupt. Her head lifted. 'He couldn't face up to the consequences of what he'd done.'

She breathed in deeply and he knew that there was only this opportunity.

'What had he done?'

She looked square at him again but now the beseeching had faded. Yet there was a sense that having gone this far it was only fair . . .

'There was a history to it.' Grace was regaining her caution. 'Father was bad with him. And he couldn't handle drink. There were a couple of scrapes. Leonard managed them but it couldn't go on. He should never have married her. A pleasant little body, from the Newcastle side, sent over here to live with some aunt up in the hills. She was a very good-looking lass – you couldn't deny that. And there was something about her – quiet, but she had Ellen's smile about her. He fell hook, line and sinker, of course, and he could charm the birds off the trees when he wanted to. Leonard thought she would be the making of him because he did adore her at first and there was such a lot that was good in him.' Her head tilted back, just slightly, as if she were swallowing imminent tears. She looked at Sam as if he were an inquisitor. 'I'll tell you no more. Leonard tried his best. But he ran away. A card now and then at Christmas and that was it.' She looked out of the window but by now her poise was recovered. 'I never even knew he'd passed over until that Colin of his marched in. He's very like. Very like.' She paused for a while and by straining Sam heard the music from a wireless in one of the guest rooms – a sound that barely rippled in the silence. Finally she looked directly at Sam, her eyes glazed with unshed tears, and added, 'But I fear he hasn't his father's . . . good heart. No mind that he was weak.'

The words were murmured and Sam pursued it no further. He stayed on just for a while, as if he were visiting a patient in hospital and wanted to make sure that everything was settled before he left.

The cold outside caught him by the throat and a few flakes of snow twisted and swirled in the bitter wind. He clutched his jacket collar around his neck and bowed his head into the weather.

CHAPTER NINE

'They sent me a through ticket,' said Mrs Baxter. 'It means I have to set off from Wigton station.'

'Sam'll carry your cases down.' Ellen guessed that this was the reason for Mrs Baxter's uncharacteristic visit and the expression of relief confirmed it.

'If he wouldn't mind.'

'No, no.' Ellen discouraged gratitude. 'More tea?'

'No, thank you. That was lovely, thank you.'

'How long will it take?'

'Nearly three days. By the time I've changed from one thing to the other. There's people to meet you at London and on to the boat. I wish it was over with.'

'I'm sure they'll have it organised. Mary tells me she's looking forward to it.' Ellen smiled at the little girl, who was sitting deep in an armchair, her short legs just jutting over the edge of the cushion, her concentration fully trained on the farmyard she was crayoning in. Joe, thankfully, was at choir practice.

'I wish I could say the same.' Mrs Baxter blinked away the emotion that threatened and hid her face behind the cup, searching for a last sip of tea. 'But there we are,' she said, when she re-emerged.

'I see enough of them at the flicks.'

'Detectives? They can take you out of yourself. There's different varieties.'

'No.'

'Adventure type? Man against the odds sort of thing.'

'Had enough of that.' It was a useful excuse. Anything that helped to get him to the destination he was blind to.

'You won't want romance.'

Sam shook his head. 'I seem to be hard to please, Willie.'

'Not a bit of it.' The response was a little forced and Sam noticed.

'What are you on at present? Reading-wise?'

'Rudyard Kipling.'

'A bit kiddies' stuff,' said Willie, and Sam could not bring himself to reveal that it was the poetry so he nodded, as if agreeing, betraying the passion of the last week.

'There's always the classics,' the librarian waved a hand towards the darkest part of the room, 'over there. Charles Dickens, William Makepeace Thackeray, Robert Louis Stevenson – we've got them all on parade. There's J. B. Priestley, Somerset Maugham. More up-to-date type of thing.'

'I'll try him.'

'I should give you a Thomas Hardy as well. Just to keep the balance.'

Sam did not ask what Willie meant by that.

'And,' concluded the librarian, seeing a potential disciple and treading carefully, 'I'll throw in a bit of a kiddies' book by P. G. Wodehouse. You like cricket?'

Sam laughed.

'*Mike*, it's called. There's amusing parts in it. Now. I'll need your particulars.'

In his beautiful copperplate handwriting, Willie filled in Sam's library card and told him the rules, emphasising the fines, and even had time to give him a brisk tour of the shelves.

Sam took Joe along to the library the next time although by now the boy much preferred to go on his own. Ellen had taken him with her for a year or so. She liked to have a romance on the go and Mr Carrick fed the boy unhurriedly from the small but adequate selection of his 'kiddies'' books, one of which was *Mike*.

CHAPTER THIRTEEN

It was on the Saturday that Ellen had gone to Carlisle with Joe and Colin to see *Great Expectations*.

Annie came to their house, her first visit, and when Sam opened the door, she said, 'He's gone on the tramp, Sam.'

Speed and his two brothers stood some distance away, across the yard, next to the cold-water tap.

Annie had delivered her news, and now she waited.

'When did he go?'

'Yesterday morning. They didn't miss him till night.'

'Who said he'd gone on the tramp?'

'Me, Sam. He's been saying he would. But . . .' She had kept it to herself, another fear suppressed, another burden carried alone. Her face, rarely relieved by much colour, was lard pale, her eyes expressed misery, her sturdy shoulders slumped, hands in pockets, the cheap headscarf no protection against the rain.

'We'll find him.' Sam tried to sound optimistic.

He left a note for Ellen.

'Best if you stay at home,' he said to Annie. 'As likely as not, that's where he'll be heading. I'll go and talk to them at the hospital.'

Speed had edged forward. 'Can I come with you, Mr Richardson?'

Sam liked being part of the betting trade. He had always liked a gamble. He liked talking to the other men about the form, the going, the jockeys, the trainers, the tipsters, unjust losses, narrow wins, missed opportunities, the quality and breed of the horses. He liked the numbers, the mathematics of each ways and doubles and trebles and accumulators, the wonderful and multiple combinations of bets that a man could squeeze out of a shilling. He liked the role of transparent secret agent slipping through police lines with the coppers and the tanners and the bobs and the occasional florins and half-crowns deep in deep pockets. The illegality of this innocent bet-reaping heightened the day. And on these summer nights he liked going off to the hound trails in the countryside with the perpetually ailing Henry, chalking the odds on the board, handing out the tickets, keeping the books, being close to the nudge and rumour, racing certainties, philosophical losers, gambling men.

The luck for Ellen was that this kept Sam happily in the town most evenings until at least seven so that she could delay going back to Greenacres to make their supper. As often as not, Joe would eat with Colin and Grace. It was good for Joe too, Ellen maintained, rather stoutly, to herself. There were very few of his age on the new estate yet and in town he could keep up with his old pals. Sometimes it seemed Joe did little more than sleep over at Greenacres, and there were nights when he did not even do that, when Grace or Colin claimed him and Ellen yielded, happy enough to share her fortune.

More than any other song she could think of for years, Ellen loved 'Galway Bay', which was all over the wireless. Bing Crosby's crooning sorcery seeped into Ellen's mind like a lullaby, a soothing sealing song of hope realised, down among the anonymous, those 'scorned just for being what we are', a song of simple powers and pleasures – the sun setting, the moon rising, and all that could be discovered plain there before you, you only had to reach out, could even catch a penny candle on a star. In those first months at Greenacres, it became her signature tune and when she hummed it she felt the world was good, and luck was on her side.

CHAPTER SIXTEEN

'Still no new P. G. Wodehouse?'

'Still no new P. G. Wodehouse.'

'Popular fella,' said Sam, gloomily.

'Surprisingly,' Willie Carrick admitted as he signed Sam off on a collection of short stories by Guy de Maupassant, recommended by the librarian as the French answer to Somerset Maugham.

'He just makes me laugh,' Sam explained, apologetically. He had read the P. G. Wodehouse books at least twice on the first borrowing and occasionally reborrowed them a few months later. They had become a happy addiction. That alternative universe, with its constellations of brilliant butlers and great houses, barmy aunts, true lovers, common-touch eccentric aristos and amiable brainless wonders had ensnared him and there were sentences he wanted to read aloud. They delivered so many shades of pleasure, laughter was often the least of it. He had pressed Willie to call in reinforcements from Central Stack but Central Stack so far had not responded to the call.

'Short stories,' said Willie, pushing the Maupassant across the table, 'rather leave me cold. Except the dialect, but that has another interest in it. You've just got into them and then they finish, type of thing.'

The boy looked from one to the other, panting now with fear, hope to die, his daddy who could always terrify him now tall as a tree and set-faced with anger, cross my heart, his mammy talking in that funny voice as if she might start to cry, she never cried.

'Just tell us,' said Sam, trying hard to be calm, but with no great success.

'I didn't pinch it,' he heard himself speak. It helped to speak. 'I didn't pinch it, Mammy, I didn't pinch it.'

'Tell us where you got it!' Sam's voice rose again. 'Just *tell* us!'

'I didn't pinch it. I didn't. I didn't pinch it. I didn't.'

Ellen reached out to put an arm around his shoulders but Joe evaded her and stood up and backed over the Meccano, trampling on it, noticing, could not do anything to mend it, backing away, hope to die.

'You must have got it somewhere!'

Sam moved towards the boy and Ellen was on her feet between them. Joe was now babbling into a scream.

'I didn't pinch it. I promise. I promise. I didn't pinch it.'

'Why won't he answer?'

'Why won't you tell us, Joe?'

The boy was now against the wall.

Sam suddenly stepped past Ellen, picked him up high and shook him.

'Where – did – you – get – that – bloody – money?'

'Sam!'

'I didn't pinch it, Daddy. I didn't. Daddy! I didn't. I didn't pinch it! Cross my heart! Hope to die! Hope to die! Cross my heart!'

The words were screamed.

'Sam!'

Joe broke into terrible sobs. Held high. His body shaking.

Slowly, Sam lowered him to the ground.

He nodded to Ellen, who came over and hugged the child now buckled with grief.

Sam went back to his chair and waited for it to stop. Ellen took Joe into the kitchen for a cup of water. When after a little time she brought him back she was holding his hand tightly. The boy was still not quite over the sobbing.

'I believe him,' said Sam, rather hoarsely, staring at Ellen as if not seeing her. 'I don't know how he came by it. But I believe him. I believe you, Joe. You didn't pinch it.'

Joe looked through the blur of water, his face simply aching for approval. Sam took a deep breath. 'It'll be your secret, then, Joe. Everybody can have secrets.'

Tears came again, but unconvulsive now, tears that the storm had passed.

And then a magnificent thing happened. Something which Joe would cherish throughout his life. Something which he could never have imagined or dared to dream of. A greatness.

'Tell you what,' said Sam. 'You give your face a wash. Better use cold water. And clear this Meccano up. And we'll all three go and see the second house. How about that? Upstairs. Posh seats. OK?'

And that is what they did.

In the cinema, Joe sat between them, erect and attentive as a soldier on guard. Now and then Sam glanced at him and saw that every word was being mouthed noiselessly. Once, Joe returned the glance with a look of such gratitude that Sam remembered another look, long ago now, when he had returned from Burma and given the boy the painted wooden train with three carriages.

He carried him most of the way home. A few minutes along the road, through the lines of the old town, Joe had just gone. The soft weight of him. Bringing him back.

CHAPTER EIGHTEEN

On a cold Saturday afternoon in June, the orphans came to the park as they did most Saturday afternoons. The boys had cropped hair. The girls' cut was matchingly severe. There was a cheapness and uniformity about the drab clothes that further distanced them and they tended not to mix. After the first flush of arrival they moved in rather a desultory, dutiful fashion between the banana slide, the swings, the roundabout and the long plank of the American swing. They were always under the supervision of two nuns who escorted the crestfallen crocodile through the town, one leading, one following.

On a Saturday afternoon in June, even a cold one, the serious bowling men were out for a league game in full white force on the lovingly mown green and the two tennis courts, again sporting white, boasted their usual patient Saturday queue. The putting green had just been established. It was not a great draw. Few wanted to waste their money on it. The orphans had no money.

Over the summer weeks, Joe had struck up a friendship with two of the orphans. Both were older than he was. Xavier was as tall as Speed, black-haired, gaunt, big-knuckled; Billy was more Joe's height but broader, very white-faced, a gap between his front teeth. Both were passionate in their friendship for Joe who was deeply attuned to

'Want to go for a walk upstreet?' Joe held his tongue, appealed to Ellen. 'Walking upstreet,' Colin repeated bitterly. 'The poor man's Saturday night out.'

Joe had planned to track down the Market Hall gang, failing that to seek out Speed, now spindly tall and drifted away from his chief acolyte. He did not want to walk upstreet with Colin and his hesitation revealed that too clearly.

'Not Joe as well?' Colin cried and he turned to Ellen as to a judge.

'You'll go with your uncle Colin,' Ellen said.

'Colin,' Joe corrected her.

'You can't force the lad.' He nicked the cigarette and put it back in the packet. 'I'll go on my own. I've got plenty of friends in Wigton. Not everybody wants me gone.'

The desperation beneath the bravado touched Ellen. She was all he had. He had no one else. No one close. Not even Grace, who seemed to fear him. In his sad-eyed petulance she saw a call for help and she had no alternative. He was her father's son and she had adopted him as her own and would never let him down. She could see the deep well of weakness and maybe her father had been like that.

She got her purse and took out five shillings. She held it out to him but talked to Joe. 'We all want Colin to stay in Wigton, don't we, Joe?'

'Yes,' said the boy, laconically, hoping he did not have to go upstreet.

'I'll let the lad find his old playmates,' said Colin, pocketing the cash, happily bribed to instant contentment. He took up a boxer's stance and jabbed out a left. Joe parried and they shadow-boxed each other for a few moments.

'Freddie Mills is never going to be a world champ!'

'You wait,' Joe said.

'I can't.' Colin's reply was delivered as a stroke of wit. 'I'm off upstreet!'

'Can I go out?'

'Yes,' Ellen said, although she would have given a lot to have had Joe stay, just to be there, as she felt the events of the day lining up to distress her.

—⟋⟋⟍—

On Sundays, Ellen would see Sam's unmarried sister Ruth. The women appreciated each other more the more they met. Ruth looked so like Sam – the very tone of the copper hair, the blue eyes, quick movements and occasionally a gesture so precisely similar that Ellen would laugh aloud and say, 'Sam does that. Exactly that,' and it brought them even closer.

She went down to the cottage next to the park trailing Joe who had been allowed to change out of his Sunday clothes – no matter the cassock covered all in the choir – into his school clothes, an act of charity enabling him to play in the park without disabling guilt. The park was always a plus for Joe, and his aunty Ruth would produce a cake and most likely a bottle of pop, which his mother would insist on paying for, and Joe would drift out of earshot of their gentle argybargy. The minus was that he had to sit in the little front room for at least half an hour before he was set free and there might be nobody in the park he could gang up with and his grandfather tended to commandeer him for a job even on a Sunday.

But his grandfather had gone down into West Cumberland to visit another of his daughters.

'I think he went to look for work,' said Ruth.

They were having tea. Joe was sucking at his pop. He had eaten the bread and jam. He had to wait for the interminable grown-ups to finish theirs before he would be allowed a bit of that icing cake.

'What about this?' Ellen looked in the direction of the park.

'He's frightened it'll go.' Ruth's fine handsome face wore an enigmatic half-smile when she felt obliged to explain her father. 'The council says it's broke. They can't do anything about that death-trap past the bridge beside the Show Fields. They can't put in the phone boxes they promised either. They just had the money to clean the beck beside the factory. Dad's convinced it's him next.'

'Does he have to work?'

Ruth shrugged.

'You can have the cake now,' she said.

'You can take it out with you if you like,' Ellen added, sensing that Ruth wanted a private exchange.

Joe catapulted from the room.

'I'll never be able to convince him that I don't want to put him in the workhouse as he still calls it. Whatever I say. He thinks moving into Wigton is part of a plan of mine. He knows that we had to move. We were lucky to get this place.'

With care and ingenuity Ruth had managed to redeem the old cottage and give it a brief last life.

'There's something else,' Ruth said, later. She had rehearsed it but it made no difference. The strength of this early-middle-aged woman that had kept her father's paranoia from breaking point, the assurance of this loyal daughter who had shared her loneliness and his fears through several thousand nights of intense cohabitation and intense separateness, none of this helped as she stammered: 'There's somebody. There's . . . there's somebody I'm seeing.'

'Ruth!'

Ellen wanted to cheer but knew it would stifle her with

embarrassment. Out of her own suppressed delight she hoped she sounded casual.

'Do I know him?'

'He's from Maryport.'

'Where did you meet him?'

'At the pictures! In Maryport. I was seeing Marjorie and there was time in hand. He sat next to me and we got talking in the interval.'

'Well.' Ellen's sigh was deep in satisfaction. 'I'm really pleased. I'm really pleased. He's a lucky man.'

'I'm the one who's lucky.' Ruth's response was so earnest that it gave Ellen the chance to laugh aloud.

'Is he serious?'

'Yes.' Ruth's expression was surprise, even wonder. 'Although we can't see each other much at present because of his work. He's a salesman.'

'With a car?'

'With a car.'

'Ruth Richardson!'

'But Dad,' she said, fighting off the elation that Ellen's transparent pleasure provoked, 'he's found out and he thinks I'll leave here.'

'You might have to.'

'He could come.'

'What does your – what's he called?'

'Frank.'

'Frank think about that?'

'I haven't raised it.'

'Don't rush it.'

'I keep thinking I should.'

'Not yet . . . I'm so pleased, Ruth.' She emphasised each syllable, heavily. 'I am so pleased.'

Bevan. "The Tories are lower than vermin," he says. That's a terrible thing for a man to say in this country. Who's lower than Nye Bevan? Nothing but jumped up.'

'Now then!' Grace reached for her old impaired command and did indeed recover enough of it to subdue her husband.

'Nye Bevan,' said Mr Kneale, whose fair-mindedness in all such matters would never be compromised, 'will turn out to be as great a man of peace as Winston Churchill was in the war. "From the cradle to the grave" is a more worthy remark of Bevan's, Leonard. I agree about the vermin, distasteful.' And his moon face pinched with a representation of distaste. 'But for what he is doing for the health and general benefit of the people, there will be monuments, Leonard, and I speak as a Liberal.'

'No more politics,' said Grace, exploiting her unexpected ally skilfully.

—ɱ—

Ellen walked back to Greenacres, revelling now in the warm evening, still light, those on the streets softer-mannered because of the warmth, telling each other how warm it was, how good it was to be warm at this time of day, how this was more like the thing.

Sadie spotted her as she was passing the Fountain and broke away from the group she was with. 'We were just walking up and down,' she said. 'No dance tonight. Typical.'

They walked along the West Road and Ellen let Sadie do most of the talking while she watched the last emberings of the red sky. To Ellen a bonus of the walk to the new estate was that she would catch sunsets, plain and huge before her as she came down the hill and looked towards the sea, to Silloth and other resorts where the sunsets were famous. She loved them. When she had gone cycling with Sam before the war they had sought out romantic spots – in the Lake District, along the Roman wall, into Scotland – not only to do their courting but for the beauty of the place, soaking themselves in it.

Sadie walked her back all the way. No one was in. They had a cup of tea and then Ellen set Sadie back down to the bridge. Even by that time, it was still light, deep purplish shade on the small hills lapping the town.

'It said on the wireless it was eighty-eight degrees in Carlisle cemetery today,' Sadie announced. 'Some of them'll think they've been put in the wrong spot!'

'Too hot for me,' Ellen confessed to her trustworthy friend.

'Can't be hot enough for me,' said Sadie, and the sun had more deeply tanned her always brown skin. 'I could live in Africa. Same tomorrow, it said.'

'They're not always right.'

'They will be tomorrow. "Red sky at night: shepherd's delight." I thought you'd have noticed it.'

Ellen watched Sadie begin up the hill and then turned for home.

Speed gathered his gang early. Joe had gone down to the Show Fields as on other holiday mornings to fish for sticklebacks under the bridge but he followed Speed without demur, unafraid. Speed had shot up in height, left Joe far behind, moved into a gang of bigger boys, too big for Joe, but Speed let him join.

The half-dozen of them padded through the long-grassed summer fields upstream alongside the serpentine Wiza river, through one kissing gate, through another until they came to the third Show Field and the object of Speed's purpose. There was a dam built a few score yards downstream from the bridge, almost opposite Pasce Egg Hill. It turned a natural pool into a deep luscious bathing hole, black water until the sheltering alders and willows. Three boys were there adding yet more height to the stoutly constructed barrier.

They pretended to ignore Speed and his gang but it was no help. Joe was in total ignorance of what was about to happen. He was bewildered by the ferocity of the attack. The three boys ran. Speed and the others, Joe belatedly joining in, broke up the dam. They broke it up with dedication. They used the larger stones to batter the patiently patted mud and pebbles and branches that had held the wall. They carried the bigger stones down-river and dumped them in a small deep pool. They destroyed it. 'We need this water,' said Speed, who led them at a gallop chanting, 'We are Kit Carson's men,' back into the first Show Field.

Here was the best place. As the river swayed between the soft sandy banks in this first field, the popular field, the field of circuses and football, it had carved out a deep swathe, a little bay. Here, traditionally, in such hot weather, the big dam was built and those who built it owned it.

By midday it was well founded and they raced to their homes for dinner. Ellen made sandwiches for Joe to take back with him after hearing a bowdlerised version of the building of the dam. She herself had swum there, in years before the war and as she sheltered from the heat of the glowing hot day, she remembered with affection that tang of river water, the coolness of it after lying on the grassy bank, the free amiable anarchy of the boy-made pool.

Word went out. It became a little resort, a spa, an adventure. Speed and some of the bigger boys made a raft. Smaller boys braved the trickle of water on the wrong side of the dam and hopped across stones on the river-bed. One or two of the bigger boys ran hard across the grass and leaped and bombed the water. Joe loved swimming and was developing pace in the front crawl. Here he was reduced to the breast-stroke, more sedate, but more able to look around and avoid being bombed.

There was a girl there, who had just moved into the estate. She had come from a knot of houses in the East End, cottages just one up from mud and wattle, thrown together for weavers in the previous century. Joe had caught her eye more than once in the Easter holidays when they were playing around the half-built houses, chasing games, hiding games, easily converted into the obscure excitement of en-counters. Then she had largely disappeared again, to the Catholic school. Now she was here, with her mother, but her mother was absorbed in conversation with another woman and it seemed to Joe the girl slipped away especially for him and together they played around the raft, a private game of tag, of touch, of splashing each other and showing off (him), switching from chaste to the occasional stun of flirtation (her), she in her red bathing suit covered in little blobs waiting to be popped, he in his over-large black woollen trunks held up by his snake belt, white-skinned both, larky, superficially innocent, making a month out of the long, slow, hot hours of a boon day.

The dispossessed gang came late, after the crowd had moved away, hoping that Speed and his gang had been drawn off with them, but Speed had waited.

The invaders scaled across the river along the fence that spanned the bridge beside the kissing gate. The numbers were about even. Speed and the others picked up as many throwable pebbles as they could find. There was plenty of ammunition.

The raiders fired the first stone. The early volleys were careful. The boys sought protection from the uneven land and squirmed flat between the necessary boldness of leaping up to aim and fire. Most of these were boys of twelve, thirteen, strong enough now to make the stones rifle across the evening tranquil water that lay between them. Joe and Ed, another smaller one, had been dispatched to the wall itself, which gave them more protection but also – Joe reckoned – opened them to the brunt of any frontal attack on the dam.

Speed began to work his way up-river. He was still wearing nothing but the handed-down pair of his father's army underpants that served as a costume. His spurt of growth had made him even leaner. This long-distance battle was getting nowhere, relying on a lucky hit, not frightening enough. He crossed the river.

But they had used his desertion from the main force to begin what Joe dreaded, a move towards the dam and now there were three of them almost there, stones hailing down as if by windmill arms. Joe knew one thing and that was that you did not run away. There was nothing else in his head as the confidence and war whoops of the enemy grew stronger and Speed, out-manoeuvred, found himself stuck behind a tree, attacked steadily and with accuracy by two of the three remaining invaders. The small section of his own forces left on the bank seemed frozen in their posts, held down by the single fire directly opposed to them over the water.

The enemy started hacking at the dam. Speed saw it and stepped out but a stone welted into his shoulder, another hit the slender tree. These were good shots. He stepped back. He needed more ammo. Meant going further back. On to the riverbank.

Ed worked his way along the dam towards the raiders and Joe had to follow him. The other gang were loosening the end of the wall and the water was trying to flow. Ed looked at Joe and nodded and Joe understood that he had to follow Ed. The bigger boy took a breath and then yelled and stood up, as high as the parapet, and scrambled on to

229

confessing failures, revealing unfulfilled ambitions, and the more Sam and Ellen were trusted, the more lives were uncovered before them. They became secular confessors.

For Sam the pub would serve. It could be a world. It was world enough. It would take care of Ellen and Joe. It would make sure that his father got a regular free drink. Colin had shown willing: for Ellen's sake there might be a chance for him. He could master it, make the work work for him. He had felt the glove fitted from that first encounter with Mrs Hewson and every day confirmed it.

Only Ellen could undermine it and he watched her carefully. He knew that she would not set out to thwart him but there was no doubt that her dislike of the idea of a pub was real. He was asking a lot.

Ellen saw that this was his deal. In years not old, just entering his fourth decade, she knew, she could see it in every move he made, that this was his destination. This was the man she had married before the war but it was also someone else, forever that distance apart, forever following his own drum not so much unwilling as unable to share everything as once they had so long ago, in another life.

The pub depressed her. She was young. She wanted the normal things – dances, evenings, the same rhythm as others. But now she was a landlady. The word made her cringe. Every association of the word made her cringe despite her respect for at least three of the landladies in the town. But they were on a bigger scale than she was, she thought, and older, more capable of standing up to the job. For the first time in her life she feared she might not be up to a task and the feeling was a clammy morning sickness, a burden.

But it had to be borne. Sam had called on her loyalty. The best had to be made of a bad job. Private reservations had to be excised. They were a luxury. At times she thought she would weep all day but she stayed dry-eyed and the tears only stained her mind. It taxed her, though, this doing against her will, and Joe was sidelined, left to shift for himself, given the odd treat where there had been attention. Sam too withdrew from the boy, locked into a new and demanding life.

Ellen found that work helped numb feeling. Cleaning was imperative, cleaning downstairs, on the stairs, in the flat, wanting but having to wait for new wallpaper, new lino, new paint, cleaning a grease-coated stove, a brown-stained sink, opening hours, midday, then tidy up, shop for tea, opening hours again, she had to learn to do the bar while Sam went out to see to the buses for the hounds or take a break, learn the prices, pull a pint. Men were different in a pub: a pub was the extension of their house yet it was her home, especially the kitchen, where they could be having supper, her and Joe, and people would just come in with a drink, for the fire and the company. All the settlement of family at Greenacres blown away, blown far away, never to be lived again. The pub, her home, known as the House. Sam kept a good House.

She paid Sadie to help with the cleaning every morning and that was a blessing. Sadie loved the excitement of the newness. Sadie found Jack Ackerman, Jack Ack, to play the accordion on Friday night and Saturday night. Jack could accompany anything. Never had a lesson. All the old songs. And the new – 'Galway Bay', of course, and 'Woody Woodpecker', 'I'm Looking Over a Four Leaf Clover'; give Jack Ack a couple of lines and he could vamp his way through. Sadie herself was better than the wireless, Ellen thought. Scarcely a film star moved or an American singer sang a note without a salty report from Sadie. 'Air freshener,' she cried in those first few days, 'give us bags of air freshener and we'll make this pub into a holiday camp, Ellen – just you wait and see, like Mr Asquith said.'

Colin was found jobs. Sam paid him a few bob even though he could have done the jobs himself. Ellen saw that as an act of love for her. Colin felt that at last Sam respected him. He bloomed, Ellen reported to Grace, who pleased Ellen by agreeing that she could see it. It would be the making of him. He got himself a crew-cut, which Ellen said did not suit him at all but it was part of a new start, and she could understand that.

The first months were dirty, tiring daily drudgery and the only way to get through was to chatter to Sadie and think about something else all the time. Sam took on the cleaning of the outside lavatories, for which Ellen was grateful. He would try to avoid asking her to serve in the pub at midday through the week – except for the ten minutes he took for his dinner. He tried as best he could to ease the bruise of the disappointment she tried to conceal and ignore.

The curious thing was that Ellen became as big an attraction as Sam. Her admonishments to young men that they were wasting their money on a second pint and should save up instead; her warm welcoming of the Salvation Army selling *War Cry* and the *Tower* on Saturday nights; the pleasant women friends she asked in to help serve in the Singing Room and the Darts Room at weekends; above all, the deep and deepening knowledge she held, and the quiet passion she had for all the doings of the town, brought in its own number who would say not, 'I'm off to Sam's House,' or even 'the Blackamoor', but 'off to talk to Ellen'. And as time went on, these conversations, this court of contact, become a balm.

Sam and Ellen flared up with each other still, but now there was the distorting pressure of others. A confrontation had to be instantly defused when a customer called and the anger of personal passion was immediately masked by a necessary politeness, an imperative sense of privacy, which exacerbated the anger, shovelled insult on it by demeaning it.

There were glimpses. There were moments. Ellen would see Sam, standing at an empty bar in the first opening hour of many a weekday. He would be studying form in the paper or doing his books, smoking a cigarette, the hair still deep copper, something about the confidence of the posture that still moved her, the completion of his appearance by the spirally smoke from the cigarette curling around the motes of dust, the sureness of the man, the man who had gone away and come back half known. And Sam found that in the busy evenings towards closing time when the orders showered in, he would be on the lookout for a smile – not directed towards him, just a real smile that would open up to him the girl he had met when she was very young, the young woman he had craved throughout the war. It gave him a chime of pleasure – that there could be happiness for her here, and in that happiness he could see what he loved.

They were never out of each other's lives. Morning, noon, night. Times of retreat were rare. Such intense cohabitation made demands they had not bargained for. Every hour was intertwined. Love was stretched too thin to cope. Disagreement had a multitude of opportunities. And yet, in that intensity, a new reliance slowly accreted, a proven sense of the two of them. Where nothing could be long disguised or ever hidden, they knew each other as deeply as any other knowing. Empathy became necessity. Tolerance had to find new limits. No mood could be consumed in secret, no slight concealed. The intensity of consistent partnership in all things on all days grafted new roles on to the boy-girl, lovers, man-wife, parents' roles they already had.

Joe ran between the two of them in a suppressed panic in those first raw, effortful, tiring weeks. The newness, the liberties, the

seven steps he crawled, a hundred-and-eighty-degree turn. Eleven steps to the gate. He pulled his body up and like a very old and ailing man he worked his way down them and into the pub, the floor cold on his feet, some light in the bar and the Darts Room from the street-light on Market Hill. He stood beside the inner door. There was the picture of the little black boy. He heard his screams but could not join in.

In the Darts Room he knelt on a chair and looked through the window at Market Hill, so much of the territory of his short life. He saw nothing but the blackness beyond the weak yellow single street-light glow and no one went by. He was cold now. His head felt so strange, so unlike him, unlike anything, only fear, nothing else, fear, fear, but he could not cry.

When he heard them coming home, he moved, though sluggishly, up the stairs, stayed on the landing.

The door opened, bringing back life, and the boy slumped. He wanted to run down but what could he say? What could he tell them? Their voices were unafraid. He dare not lean forward in case they saw him but their voices were so warm that he wanted to cry but you didn't.

When he heard his mammy say that she was going straight to bed he turned and made himself go back into his bedroom. He did not look in the corner. He waited for her to come in, and when she did, he pretended that he was fast asleep. She looked at him for a moment or two. He was too old to kiss.

CHAPTER TWENTY-EIGHT

'I feel bad about it now,' she said.

'No need.'

But he kept his back to her. They were alone in the bar mid-morning pre-opening time. Sam was at the sink rinsing some newly washed spirit measures. Ellen stood beside the pumps, like a plaintiff.

'I didn't really take in that it was a Saturday.'

'Why should that bother you?'

Ellen knew very well that he needed her to wash the glasses on Saturday of all nights yet she found not sarcasm in Sam's reply but a scrupulous attempt to let her believe her life was just as normal as that of everyone else who could take a Saturday afternoon and evening off.

'Joe's looking forward to it.'

'There you are, then.'

He turned round and any residual resentment dissolved at the sight of her. She could still move him to the heart of himself, at unlikely times these days – now, flushed in her anxiety at letting him down and yet holding on to this small proof of normality that the pub had taken from her.

'We'll manage fine. Alfreida'll help in the bar, Joyce is coming to do the Singing Room.'

'I never thought,' she said, but in the saying there was the nod, the acknowledgement that he understood the reason behind it all, and through that understanding truly understood her.

'Bad enough we take shifts for holidays.'

Ellen for a week to Ayr Butlin's with Joe, Sam unsuccessfully attempting a three-day break at Morecambe: back after two, Joe bribed into agreement with a yellow polo-necked sweater. Their first and last attempt.

He was wearing the sweater when he came into the bar.

'Did you tidy up all the crates in the back cellar?'

'Yes.'

'Here, then.'

Sam fished out two half-crowns and watched with interest as his son's face brimmed full of gratitude, lined with an innocent lust for the heavy coins.

'Thanks, Dad. Thanks.'

Dad now. Quite suddenly. Dad. Long trousers now. And, in public, Mam – Sam enjoyed the boy's pleasure and thought, How simple it is sometimes.

'Away, then. They'll go without you.'

The bus would leave from outside the church at eleven sharp to allow for a full afternoon, even though the trip to Blackpool was targeted on the evening, for the Illuminations.

'Look after your mam, now,' Sam said, as he stood on the steps.

Joe linked arms with his mother by way of an answer. Ellen felt good. Joe on her arm in that terrible yellow polo-neck but so pleased with it she said nothing.

Pleased with Sam most of all. She had seen him harden. In the first years the battle to make it a friendly house had put Sam at odds with some of the tougher men in the town and there had been times when she herself had felt the echo of it, when a walk upstreet was a small demonstration of courage and a Saturday night could be nothing but watching the fuse burn towards the explosive. It was worse, she thought, that he had bound himself never to fight. She had hated it when he had been in those few fights before the war and she would hate it again but the effort to bottle up his temper took a lot out of him, she thought, and then his anger turned on her, on Joe, on himself. But the pub meant independence and for that he would endure what came. Yet it had hardened him so his gentleness just now was not only warming in itself but a reminder of what had been, or what always would be, perhaps, a break in the clouds.

'All aboard the *Skylark*! Roll or bowl a ball!' Colin had nominated himself the life and soul of the bus. 'Joe'll sit next to me,' he announced.

Ellen was relieved to see him in such form. He had found himself a blazer – he was good at winkling out bargains, doing swaps – and this, together with his new cleanly parted, smartly Brylcreemed, unquiffed hair-cut, helped him cut something of a dash, especially among the older ladies. He helped them clamber into the coach, raincoated, scarfed, hatted, gloved, slung with sandwiches and cake and flasks, hard-saved money in the pocket marked for presents, which would be rock mostly, pink-sheathed pure white centre with BLACKPOOL stamped through in red.

Before the engine had turned the singing began.

Colin made Joe laugh with his imitation of the Goons. The boy had not met any other adult as addicted as everybody at school. Colin specialised in Eccles.

First they drove along the Front, a flourish to set the tone. Past the great music halls and theatres housing the stars that packed in thousands every day.

At the Anglican Young People's Association they had done Four Men In A Balloon. Who should be thrown out? Who was most important? The doctor, the teacher, the scientist or the vicar. Joe had been given the vicar the week before. The responsibility had weighed on him.

He was intimidated by his real vicar because the man did not like him. He never said so but Joe could tell and it bothered him. He would chuck a kind remark to other choirboys or give them a hello by name or even a compliment now and then but Joe might not have existed. Yet he worshipped God and Jesus Christ through this man whose authority was not lightly worn, whose sermons could be threatening and always freighted with names Joe did not know or complex sentences he could not comprehend. The vicar had such a graceful voice, as good as the wireless, and when he spoke the communion 'Take, eat, in remembrance of me,' Joe bred goose-bumps. When the AYPA decided on a balloon debate, he had volunteered eagerly, but drawing the vicar had spoiled it.

The vicar might not turn up. Most times he did not. That would be a big help. And yet the boy wanted the vicar to hear what he had to say – that without the vicar nobody would be able to get to know God and be saved so there would be no eternal life for anyone, and compared with eternal life what was the use of a doctor, a teacher or a scientist? Vicars healed the soul and taught the word of God and knew everything, so they were all the other three wrapped up in one. Without vicars, life was useless. You were allowed three minutes. The vicar came.

Joe stumbled as he stood in the middle of the circle of chairs, but he kept his head enough to make his points although he all but ran out of breath at the end. The vicar was asked to judge and gave it to the scientist but along the way he said that Joe had tried hard and gave him a smile. The boy was well pleased.

The sense of pleasure buoyed him up to the fish-and-chip shop where he bought his supper, sixpenn'orth with scrams, and took his time wandering down the High Street savouring the long soft chips speckled with the hard chippings of batter. It was a good moment.

Street lights were on. McQueen stood under the light at the corner of High Street and Market Hill, staring across at the Black-amoor from which he had been barred for life. He took up this position at least once a week.

McQueen was not right in the head. He had been up in court more than once for beating his mother. In drink he went from silent sullen to yelling violent without warning. He had no friends, not even a dog. He was very thick set, deep black hair heavily oiled, rarely without his old navy blue coat. His face was swollen, the cheeks, the lips, usually a glaze of red on the skin.

'Sam Richardson's a bastard!'

Joe, who had crossed the road, stopped and faced McQueen.

'Tell him I said he's a right bastard.'

McQueen began to move towards him and Joe turned away.

'Tell him I'll get him! Tell him I'm waiting for him.'

Joe moved quickly and went through the door of the pub as if seeking sanctuary.

It was quiet.

Sam saw the boy a touch flustered and strolled out of the bar. 'How did it go?'

'I didn't win. The scientist won.'

'As long as you did your best.'

'McQueen's outside.' Joe dropped his voice and looked at the floor. 'He said – he called you names. He said he would get you.'

'He's best ignored, Joe. Just ignore him.'

'But he called you names, Dad.' He hesitated. 'I should have had a go at him, shouldn't I?'

'He's best ignored.'

'But you would, wouldn't you? If you'd been me. If he'd said that about Grandad. You'd have had a go at him, wouldn't you?'

'These things are hard to call, Joe.'

'But you would.'

'Maybe.'

'I know you would.'

Suddenly feeling quite hopeless, Joe went upstairs without first going into the kitchen. He was a coward. He was overwhelmed with grief at the realisation. He was sure his dad could tell. His predominant concern at school now was to avoid Og. He would excuse himself for the lavatory in lessons rather than risk it at playtimes. He would scan the school playing-fields for Og and the sauntering, predatory pack of 3L and tack his way far from them, trying to kid himself that he wanted to play way over there, but knowing, sick to his stomach with it, that his sole purpose was to avoid Og. Even those who thought it had taken guts to fight in the first place could bring no comfort. He knew he was a coward. He was even afraid to be alone in his own house.

He knelt by his bed and read. It had become his preferred position. That his knees hurt helped somehow. He was reading *The Grapes of Wrath* and the story almost blotted out everything from his mind save for the small cold certain feeling that he was a permanent coward now, even scared of getting into bed and turning out the light.

CHAPTER THIRTY

McQueen got on to the bus outside the library in Castle Street. Joe had spotted him from his prime position in the front seat on the upper deck and his stomach had melted at the sight. McQueen had been drinking in Carlisle, the boy could see that – no one could miss the glazed face, the stagger on to the bus and then, to Joe's alarm, the uneven clump of drunken steps announced his ascent to the upper deck. Joe froze. McQueen must have taken the back seat. Joe forced himself to try to disappear through immobility. Though the bus was quite full he felt that there was nothing and no one between McQueen and himself.

He should not have gone to the game. Sam had said he would go and watch Carlisle United with Joe and the boy had given up the chance to go up to Highmoor where some of them had made a dirt track for bikes. Then Sam had pulled out at the last minute – something to do with the dog-bus going wrong – and Joe had climbed on to the crowded Carlisle bus before he could reorganise his forces. He had not found anyone to latch on to. It was a cold feeling going through the children's turnstile knowing that you would meet up with no one you knew on the other side. Somehow he had not been able to lose himself in the game. He had hurried back from the ground, taking

'You think Colin's . . .' Ellen paused, aware now that, quite suddenly, she was ready to do battle, but for what reason? '. . . no good.'

'I never said that.'

'You did. Right at the start. Right at the very beginning. How could I ever forget? When he first came. You said he was no good.'

'That was then, Ellen. That was then.'

'Now isn't any different, though, is it? You'll blame Colin for this, more than Sadie, and more than that terrible husband of hers.'

'I'll see him if you want. It'll do no good. It could make things worse. But, if you want, I'll see him.'

'It won't do any good. Not in that mood.'

'What do you want, Ellen?'

'We can't even manage a holiday together. Not even a couple of days.'

'Who would look after this place?'

'Others manage. You've taken him to Morecambe for two days, I traipse off to Butlin's.'

'You like it. You both like it.'

'Oh, yes. I like it well enough. But that isn't the point, Sam, is it?'

'He's lucky to get a holiday. What set this off?'

'This place doesn't suit a family, Sam.'

'He likes it. He can bring his pals in to play darts when we're closed. They meet up in the kitchen and play around in the stables. It has a lot of interest, a pub.'

'For you maybe. It jars on him.'

'It jars on you, you mean. That hasn't gone away.'

'I haven't complained.'

'You don't need to.'

'We only meet when we're worn out, Sam. We see each other when everybody else has drained off every bit of life there is in us.'

'It'll get better. You always have to work hard building up a business.'

'It's built up.'

'You have to watch it all the time.'

'I think,' Ellen spoke with particular care, 'that it's a way to make a living together but not live together. Not really together.'

Sam closed the book.

'What do you think everybody else does? Jack or Alfreida and Frank or Grace and Leonard for that matter or most of them. What do they do?'

'They sit down together across a fire. They listen to the wireless like we used to. They go for walks like we used to. They go to the pictures together not in single file, and holidays, even if it's only a couple of days, and Saturday afternoon and Sundays off.'

'Granted. But what do they really do? Does this all make them more interested in each other? Does this make them more interested in life? I can't see it on their faces. I can't see it in their eyes, Ellen. As often as not I can see boredom, even desperation, but most times just a putting up with it.'

'What's wrong with putting up with it?'

'Because – because you're on a lead, you're on a leash.'

'We're on a leash. Opening hours, getting ready, waiting on, waiting on everybody who turns up, having to be cheerful whatever you feel like, not being able to be quiet or a bit down, we're at everybody's beck and call, aren't we, Sam? Isn't that a leash?'

'Is that the way you see it?'

There was hurt in his question and she did not want to hurt him more but driven, this rare time, and not knowing why.

'Yes it is,' and added, but as an obvious sop, 'mostly.'

362

'It all comes back to Colin, doesn't it?' Bitterness, for the first time, no more than a touch, but marked.

'You're so uneasy with him.'

'I'll tell you something, Ellen. Now listen. Quite simple. I try my level best with Colin. In fact, if there is such a thing, I try better than my best because of you. That's all I want to say about Colin. And as for the rest, I think you're just romantic about other people's lives. We have company on our doorstep. We have talk every night. We have a bit of money to spare now. The work's hard but what work isn't? At least we get the direct benefit. And nobody bosses us about.'

'You used to be romantic. You used to talk about wanting night classes and trying to be a village schoolteacher. You were the romantic one, Sam, not me.'

'Well, that had to pass.'

'Maybe Joe'll do some of that for you.'

'You live your own life.'

'He's a good reader.' And the piano, she wanted to say, but she had said enough.

'He'll have to make a better fist of it than he's doing at the moment,' Sam said.

Ellen experienced a shadow of recognition, a dark presence inside Sam's words, brushing against her awareness of her son, disturbing her. 'What do you mean?'

He's running scared, Sam wanted to say. I can see it plain. The boy is scared. Sam had seen it enough times. And what followed fear was unpredictable save that it was bad, a lessening.

'Has he told you something's wrong?'

'He's said nothing.'

Sam's smile, which was a smile of recognition for the boy's silence, reassured Ellen sufficiently for her thoughts to revert to Colin

363

CHAPTER THIRTY-FIVE

His bedroom resembled a cell. You came in, the single bed was jammed against the wall on the left; about as much space again made up the width of the room. Beyond the bed were three items of furniture: a small chest of drawers, a wardrobe and a three-shelved bookcase. The floor was lino – red and yellow squares. The curtains were yellow and flowery. The wallpaper was also ornamented with flowers. Out of the window he saw Market Hill on which there was always, in daytime, some movement. The buses now used it, which was illegal, said Mr Carrick, Market Hill belonged to the people of Wigton. Beyond the hill he could see the fields behind which lay the baths. There was a telephone box directly across from the pub and a street-light.

Somewhere in his mind he realised – in a fragile, intermittent, all but blind manner – that this room was where he had to fight. If he could not brave being here alone without running out to the stairs or being in a locked terror, if he could not hold his ground here, then there was no hope.

He did not realise this in any worked-out way. There was no plan. Sometimes there were days on end when hostilities ceased. Usually, though, over the next eighteen months to two years, he was, in so far as he was able, fighting it through in that room.

It was easy not to go on long solitary bike rides. It was not hard to avoid windows and mirrors, although even the merest accidental reflection could unbolt him now. His name was still so strange to look at but there were few occasions when he had to.

It was the night which was always waiting for him, the night and that time just before sleep when the attack, if it were on, would begin.

He would come up to the room as late as possible, rush his prayers, still dressed, change in the bathroom, come back and be in bed so fast he would beat it. Sometimes it worked. Or go up very early, with his supper on a tray, put on the wireless, find music, have a book, read until he was heavy-headed, read beyond that, let the story become a world that filled his head, with the music, so he could feed on them when the tiredness forced him to turn to sleep. If he could think about the book and replay the music in his head then that was better than a fortress. The light left on. But there would always be a time when it was turned off.

Spring and summer helped, the curtains left partly open, the window open too so that voices from outside, clear voices outside the room, not the seethe of noise below which was part of the room, helped distract him. But as summer nights lengthened his mother and father would go for walks after closing time and he would always be awake for that and, flat on his back, try to walk with them, to be with them down Burnfoot, into Birdcage Walk, past West Cumberland Farmers, alongside Toppin's Field and Toppin's Farm, past the police station, up the long incline of Station Road, round the Blue Bell, back into the High Street towards Market Hill and the Blackamoor, going step by step with them, trying not to rush, trying not to move, untensed only when the key turned in the door and he heard a voice.

As the months went on he made it harder for himself because otherwise he would never win. He said he wanted to do his homework in his room and not in the kitchen where everybody came in and out. Homework was not now the chore that had much taxed him. He would force himself to sit alone and do it and lock himself in. In the room. He did not have the remotest idea why this action would help but he did it.

Testing himself was good. Not just in straight competition like swimming but seeing if he dared go out of the bathroom window and climb up the steep pitch of roof under which the spirit of the blackamoor boy might still be enraged. Get to the peak. Then sling himself over, let himself slide down the steep pitch, which ended in a long drop on to the concrete front of the pub, see how his nerve held, feel the terror, feel welcome sweat to the palms, begin an insect-like back sprawl upwards, his throat choking.

Testing himself. In the Scouts. In school. Though he had blankings and an overgrasping nervousness that could misfire, he wanted the tests, the tests made his head feel occupied. At the church youth club, to debate harder, dance better, show off more; in rugby to rush with the scrum, disguising the fear of tackling under the puff of effort; how long it took him to do this, go that distance, tests. Save for the choir when testing was pointless, but what reward for that pointlessness! A calm in the mind that made him feel safe, normal, in touch with the heart of whatever he was. Something of the same in reading, particularly when the book's characters took him into their skins, the story of the book became his story, he twinned with these invented people whose paths were certain sure compared with the amoeba and sludge of his own.

Envy sprouted everywhere. Everyone he liked had more that he liked than he had. And none of the fears he had. How could they be so certain of everything? He tried to drive the gang to feats of cohesion difficult for a mixed bunch of half a dozen boys not even in the same class, different tastes, talents, but they had to be together so that he could feel the solidity. Jealousies came from that, all signs of independence were proofs of betrayal, it was hopeless and endless, above all, it was endless.

Somewhere inside, to meet this perpetual threat that scooped him out, stripped the skin from inside his head, took his soul from him, abducted all but the thing of body, he had to build a redoubt. His father had told him about the redoubt, the final place. Where you had to fight until you dropped but also where you could build to win. He was seeking to build that, or a shell, but inside himself not outside. A shell to seal in that which left him, a place almost independent of his body as the inner flask of a vacuum. Blindly he stumbled towards that.

There was a terrible violence in his head. When he heard the preliminary murmurings of disruption from downstairs, he wanted to take a sword and slice them open from head to belly, those who threatened. At the boxing matches in Carlisle he liked the blows to land and growled and yelled in the crowd as deep in it as any, losing his singleness as in the choir but finding blood not peace. His feelings even for the gang could be savage, and he held on as if an unbroken horse were trying to buck him and sometimes he could not hold on and the anger uncoiled would be disproportionate, silencing, puzzling to others and leaving Joe himself dazed.

All he really knew was that he had to keep it secret, not a hint, not a sign to anyone at any time no matter what, he had to conceal the shame. And all he also knew was that he could not give in. He was beaten, he could see that when, for all his tactics, he was still prey, still defeated; but somehow being beaten had to be got through.

In this long time, when the wait of a day for the night's battle could seem like a month and despite all the furies on the surface the depths seemed not to stir but hold a sullen grip on him, there were times of escape, vivid release, a bare intensity of seeing whether a wood or a sky, a candle in the church, stones clear on a river-bed or the face of a girl in the street, to be haunted by him, however hopelessly, it was a mercy.

But he deserved no mercy, because he lied. He lied about himself and what he did in any and every way to protect the secret of what he feared. His contempt for his courage grew as the months went by. You were not frightened of such insubstantial things. You were not yellow-bellied in front of what could not even be talked about for fear of laughter. But the attacks continued and the chasm in his life was covered over as best he could with a desperation of energy that could see a whole day's reparation ripped away in moments as what was him left the body, left it petrified, vanishing into the infinite blackness for eternity unless he could be forgiven.

So she would be told. She sat very very still.

'There's a hundred and one ways to dress it up, Ellen, but to get to the point he walked out a week or two before you were born. Grace always wanted to say it was after because she thought that was nicer. It was before you were born.' He glanced at her and then quickly glanced away. No one was in sight but he dropped his voice.

'It was never a good match for either of them,' he said, 'one of those moments of madness that happens but then they were stuck with it. Except it worked itself into your father, it worked itself into him to such an extent that he could not bear to look at the poor woman – and she was bonny, nice, she was a very nice woman, your mother – but he just couldn't, well, I won't say he couldn't stand the sight of her, but that's how she must have taken it. He couldn't conceal it. Others do. And he couldn't live with it. Others have to. Whatever I said was listened to but made no odds. I was sorry for both of them. It was a terrible thing. He tried to be guided by Grace, he thought the world of Grace, but, poor fellow – and I did feel sorry for him even though what he did was a bad and a weak thing – he had a weak side, he knew that himself and he couldn't see it through. So he bolted.'

Ellen sucked her upper lip into her mouth and gripped it hard with her teeth and at the same time she nodded, again and again, only it was not only her head but slightly, stiffly even, her body, from the waist, nodding, rocking, easing the stab in her heart. There was a sound, too, a low hum, intermittent, but Leonard caught it and paused.

No one hailed them. No one passed. The sun warmed the worn sandstone church wall.

'He would send me the odd letter. He was too shamed to write to Grace save for the Christmas card. Then they dropped away. He knew he couldn't come back.'

415

'Could he not?' The words were squeezed out like a gasp.

'No,' said Leonard, as gently as he could. 'He'd burnt his boats.'

'I wish he'd come back,' Ellen whispered. 'I wish he had come back.'

Still she tried to take on the pain. Leonard dared not look at her.

'Well, Ellen. You've been a wonderful daughter to me and Grace. You have.'

'Have I?'

'We both say that.'

'Thank you.' The voice so low, now, the tone so formal.

She tried to straighten up but she could not, not yet, in a minute or so, did not want to embarrass him.

'But you see,' she said, and her voice broke completely, 'he was my father.'

CHAPTER THIRTY-EIGHT

Sam went up to Mr Kneale's quarters at six thirty as arranged. It was only the second time he had been in the comfortable set of rooms the schoolteacher had carved out of the top floor of Grace's house. The place had seemed very grand on the first visit, the widower had moved in fine furniture that had belonged to his wife and there were, everywhere, objects not seen in any other houses Sam knew. The most striking impression was that it was cluttered, pleasantly so, Sam thought, enviably so, the stacks of books and photographs, several cameras, the little tower of notes on the desk. The drink, well remembered, was the same.

'A little sherry?'

'Gladly.'

It was poured with care from a heavy decanter.

'Take a seat, Sam. Please.'

'Thank you.'

'Your very good health.' Mr Kneale.

'And to you.'

Sam quite enjoyed the sherry this time. 'Mind if I smoke?'

'I brought up an ashtray.'

'The photography still going strong then?'

'A good hobby is a friend for life,' said Mr Kneale. 'But I have to confess that this book runs it neck and neck.' He indicated the pile of notes. 'War gets you into everything.'

'I've come for some advice,' Sam said, not wanting war, stubbing the cigarette and waving away the last spiral of smoke.

'Well, I hope I can be of service.'

'It's about Joe.'

Mr Kneale was not wholly surprised. He waited.

'I suppose I'm looking for inside information.' Sam took his time. He had thought it through.

Mr Kneale nodded.

'If he was a horse I would be asking what his form was.' Sam smiled. Mr Kneale found a surer touch of real friendship in that smile than he had felt throughout his often rather wary relationship with the younger man. 'Or maybe looking for a tip.'

'I see,' said Mr Kneale.

'Leonard's found him an opening after this next year and it's very good of him. Ellen's over the moon. Joe seems quite happy. It's a job for life. Clean work.'

'Leonard says he'll take to it.'

'Did he? He should know.' Sam concentrated. What he wanted to say was that over the last months there had beat a stronger and firmer pulse in him about his son. He had begun to sense another possibility of connection.

'I always wanted to stay on at school, you know,' Sam said. He had not planned on saying that. He rushed on. 'Same as thousands. We had to leave. That was that. But when I had time on my hands in the war I thought about it. Quite a bit. Joe isn't placed like me. He could stay on, couldn't he?'

'There's provision,' said Mr Kneale. 'There is now the opportunity if the parents can afford it.'